Malin Lindroth

Train Wreck

How long does it take to wreck another person's life? Two minutes? Maybe three?

Johnny did it. He said something to her and they got together. Johnny—my *boyfriend* Johnny—and Susie P. Together, but not for real.

Except that for Susie P., it was very real. So real, she didn't even see that everyone in the hallway was bent over laughing when she and Johnny walked past, holding hands.

Johnny played with her, like a bored kid plays with a toy. But it wasn't just him. We all agreed to go along with it.

Single Voice

1 book | 2 stories

Also available in the Single Voice series

Two startling stories about the powerful impact of parents' behavior on teens

FILM STUDIES
Caroline Adderson

Cass struggles to decide what role she should play in life, an act that swallows her whole. Her movie director father is always jetting somewhere exciting, as sophisticated as Cass herself wants to be. Then along comes a school film project—and things get strange. The green light on the web cam glows like a troll's eye, and Cass knows what's been captured.

THE TROUBLE WITH MARLENE
Billie Livingston

Samantha is miserable. They used to be a family—but now it's just Sammie, and her mother, Marlene. Marlene spends her lonely days drinking wine and dreaming up the perfect suicide, while no one at school has any idea what Sammie's world is like. No one but Drew, and she's not sure she wants to let him in. Sammie wonders if Marlene is right after all. What's so great about this life, anyway?

Single Voice

1 book | 2 stories

*Two heart–wrenching tales of
sibling secrets, loyalty and loss*

I AM NOT EMMANUELLE
Carine Tardieu

Thirteen-year-old Adele impulsively
steals a pack of gum, launching her
into a rambling monologue about her
inability to live up to the "perfect" sister
who died. Convinced that her parents
would have preferred her to die instead,
Adele can't help acting out.

JUST JULIE
Nadia Xerri-L

Julie's idolized older brother is accused of
murder. When she refuses to attend his
trial, her shattered family is bewildered.
But Julie knows more about her brother
than she wants to admit, and a fateful
decision is in her hands: should she speak
the truth, or protect her family?

Single Voice

Malin Lindroth

Train Wreck

Annick Press Ltd.

Original title of the playscript: När tågen går förbi by Malin Lindroth
©2004 by Colombine Teaterförlag, Stockholm, Sweden

Series editor: Melanie Little

Copyedited by Geri Rowlatt
Proofread by Tanya Trafford
Cover design by David Drummond/Salamander Hill Design
Interior design by Monica Charny
Cover photo (boots) by Karkas / shutterstock.com

We acknowledge the support of the Canada Council for the Arts, the Ontario
Arts Council, and the Government of Canada through the Canada Book Fund
(CBF) for our publishing activities.

ONTARIO ARTS COUNCIL
CONSEIL DES ARTS DE L'ONTARIO

The publication of this work was supported by a translation subsidy from the
Swedish Arts Council.

Cataloging in Publication

Lindroth, Malin, 1965-
      Train wreck / Malin Lindroth.

(Single voice series)
Title: Train wreck, translation of: När tågen går förbi.
Title on added t.p., inverted: Too late / Clem Martini.
ISBN 978-1-55451-259-1 (bound).—ISBN 978-1-55451-258-4 (pbk.)

      I. Martini, Clem, 1956- II. Martini, Clem, 1956- . Too late.
III. Title. IV. Series: Single voice (Toronto, Ont.)

PZ7.L6596Tr 2010   j839.73'74   C2010-903491-0

Published in the U.S.A. by
Annick Press (U.S.) Ltd.

Distributed in Canada by
Firefly Books Ltd.
66 Leek Crescent
Richmond Hill, ON
L4B 1H1

Distributed in the U.S.A. by
Firefly Books (U.S.) Inc.
P.O. Box 1338
Ellicott Station
Buffalo, NY 14205

Visit our website at www.annickpress.com

I'm going to tell you exactly how it was.
I did something terrible to Susie P.

I destroyed her life. It happened so quickly.
You don't realize how quickly you can de-
stroy a person's life unless you've actually
done it. Two minutes...maybe three...that's
all it took.

I could make excuses, of course.

I could say it was a long time ago. I was young...stupid...just fifteen. I didn't know any better. That's what I've been saying to myself every day since it happened. "I was young." That's the kind of thing people say. To make themselves feel better, I suppose.

I know I have to forget it. But how can I?

It's not an easy story. It's hard to explain and probably hard to understand. But I still want to try.

Her name is Susie Peterson. But she was called Susie P. She was in my class in high school.

It was the 1980s. She'd always been there—

ever since play school. But still I couldn't say I knew her. Probably no one in our class really did.

We thought she was pretty hopeless. A real head case.

Quiet. Pale. Terrified eyes hiding behind thick bangs. And alone—she was always alone. She sat in the front row by herself, chewing her lip.

Those strange clothes she had... There were rumors about how her mother, a home-care worker, got the clothes from the old people and altered them for her daughter. But nothing was for sure when it came to Susie P.

She was the sort of person who is always the odd one out. Honestly, I can't remember a single time when I saw her with someone else. "You can work in pairs," the teachers would say. "Two people for every basket-ball!" or "In pairs in science lab." And she was always the one without a partner.

But one day—it was in ninth grade—some guys in our school decided to tease Susie P.

You could see how scared she was when they came up to her in the hallway and said they wanted to talk to her. They were the three worst guys in our school. Big guys, the kind with power. She probably thought they were going to hit her. That sort of thing did happen.

She tried to get past. But they blocked her path.

"Take it easy," one said. "We're not going to do anything to you."

"We just want to tell you that we know someone who thinks you're beautiful," said another.

Susie P. just stared at them. She didn't understand a thing.

"Come on, Susie P., wake up!" they said.

"You must know who it is."

"The guy's in love with you. At least give him a chance!"

"Just give him a chance, Susie P.!"

Everyone knew it was a joke—the whole class knew. Me, too, of course—but none of us dreamed she'd actually fall for it. I mean, no guy could really want a girl like Susie P. It would be a joke.

So we thought she would get it. But she didn't.

Instead, the girl shone. She got a kind of sparkle in her eyes like...well, like happiness, almost.

"Who is it?" she managed to say.

"We can't tell you."

"Just tell me his name..."

"You'll see who it is if you come to the football field at seven tonight."

"He wants to meet you. Come on! Give him a chance."

"Okay...okay."

She was a colossal idiot, we said, with only herself to blame. You have to understand who you are, you have to know your place, was how we thought. But that was before

I knew how far a person will go...how far she is willing to fall to feel...yes, loved. I mean...everybody wants to have someone, right? There's nothing strange about that. It's completely normal. And sometimes people do things...sick things...to keep that someone.

In that way we're alike, Susie and I.

━━ ●

Maybe it was a mistake to talk about this. Why should I dig up old stuff? She might be fine. She might have gotten over it. It might just be me.

Sometimes, though, I'm afraid she'll come looking for me, make me answer her.

That she'll want revenge.

It's stupid, I know. It's ancient history. But I can't stop thinking about it.

Maybe she doesn't even remember me. If we bumped into each other today, she probably wouldn't recognize me. That wouldn't be so strange. I don't look the same. Back then I had a perm. A really tight one, like a poodle. And electric-blue suede boots. Hideous! But that was the rage at the time.

And I wasn't exactly an angel back then.

I went around with the worst crowd. Rowdies, shoplifters, and druggies. Pretty crazy guys. I liked their attitude.

They didn't take shit from anyone.

Mom always warned me not to do what she'd done. "Don't get a husband and kids too soon. Think about your future—get an education first."

But the future wasn't my thing. It was distant, out of reach. And the more I tried to think about it, the further away it seemed.

I found it quite easy to get guys.

I always had somebody.

The year I did what I did to Susie P., I was with a guy named Johnny. He was older. He had an edge. Leather jacket with studs, lots of chains and stuff. He did exactly what he felt like doing, and I tagged along.

Sometimes, when the mood hit us, we would go into the train tunnel. When the train roared past, we would press together, tight, against the tunnel wall. So close...we could feel the rush of the wind.

It was dangerous...madness ...terrible... beautiful.

Sometimes we screamed like two crazy people when we felt the rush of the train.

I was the only girl who did things like that. I was wilder, more grown up, than the others in my class. That's what he said.

And he gave me presents. Cute stuffed animals—teddy bears and rabbits and even a gigantic tiger that I slept with every night for a while. I liked showing myself off beside Johnny in the hallways. I wanted everyone to see us, to know that we were together.

I was really in love with that guy.

I would have done anything to keep him.

They said they were only going to tease
her. It wasn't a big thing. They said it was
just a little joke, and Johnny could be part
of it. I told him I didn't like it. But he said
he wanted to be part of it. That he didn't
want to be left out.

We'd been together for three months. He'd
started talking about how we should have
sex, go all the way, so I figured it was serious,
that we really had something.

So it didn't seem fair that he was the one
who had to pretend to be interested in
Susie P. I thought someone else should do
it, someone who didn't have a girlfriend.
But he was always so afraid of letting his
friends down.

A few of us tagged along, just for laughs. We hid behind some prickly bushes while Johnny walked out onto the football field. I don't know how long she'd been waiting, but you could see she was nervous. When she saw who was coming toward her, her face started to twitch, as if she was being prodded or something—it was the shock, I guess. I doubt she ever thought the best-looking guy in school would come. She'd probably been expecting someone else. Someone more like her.

He started talking to her, in a low voice. Some garbage, lies, I couldn't hear what he said but whatever it was, it made her laugh. Then he stretched out his hand, just a little, as if he was going to touch her. The girl stood absolutely still, as if she were growing roots in the ground, and stared at his hand like she'd never seen a hand before.

And then he said it: *You're so beautiful, Susie P.* She looked completely stunned, and kept staring at his hand. I knew if we didn't show ourselves pretty soon like we'd planned, he'd have a complete meltdown.

"I'm not touching her," he'd said. And we'd all promised he wouldn't have to.

But just when I was about to get up, some jerk grabbed me and said we should wait to see what Susie P. did. We couldn't stop now, just when things were getting good.

I tried to break away but the guy wouldn't let me go. He even put his hand over my mouth.

So Johnny had to stand there, being tortured, his hand hanging in midair.

And Susie P. moved toward him. So, in the end, he was forced to touch her. To touch Susie P.

He just stood there for a second, totally stunned. Then he jerked his hand away.

My god! He gave us shit for that afterward!

━━ •

It was just a joke! Why, why couldn't she understand that? She should have seen that he wasn't serious. You can see that in a person. You feel it. Can't you?

Maybe not. She didn't.

She believed, really believed, that he might actually love her.

She changed after that. The next day, she came to school with curls and makeup, looking like somebody else. We all thought she looked absurd. It didn't suit her at all. Her lipstick was too red. Way too red! Why couldn't she see that? None of us could stop laughing.

But the worst thing was how she hung around Johnny. Followed him everywhere. In town, at school, at the burger place—there she was. It didn't matter if I was there...even if he was holding my hand! She still followed him.

Of course I got angry. Really pissed off. Anyone would.

Every time I turned around, she was right behind me, staring. Not saying a thing. Just standing there staring, waiting for him to say something...to do something.

I wanted to tell her—no, I wanted to scream it, right in her face—that she was a

disgusting little pig who should leave us
alone. Look at yourself! I wanted to shriek.
You're ugly! You wear revolting clothes
that old people have drooled in and peed
in and died in! You giggle and stare like a
moron, and you've got a whore color for
lipstick. Wake up! He doesn't want you!

But Johnny and his friends told me to
keep quiet.

They had an idea.

They said they'd changed their minds. At
first, they hadn't planned to keep the joke
going. But now that she'd started glamming
herself up, tarting herself up for Johnny,

they didn't want to stop. I said it was sick, that I didn't want to. But in the end, I went along with it.

I shouldn't be seen with Johnny, they said. We should pretend it was over between us and he should be with her instead.

They wanted to see how far they could go before she got the joke. It probably wouldn't take very long. A few days...a week, maybe.

I was afraid he would leave me. I was always afraid he would leave me.

That's how I was back then. A coward. That's what I still am, really.

▬▬ ●

We stood so close to the track in that tunnel!
So close! When the train went past. I can't
imagine what I was thinking, can't believe
I ever dared to do it. It was so dangerous.

When the train came, he held me tight.
But if he hadn't...if he had let go... I would
have been sucked out onto the rails and
killed in half a second.

Of course he never would have let go.

I trusted him.

Sometimes I tested him, though. If he stood
behind me and held my waist, I would make
my body heavy and lean on his arm...a little
more...a little more...a little more... Just to

see if what he said was true, that he would do anything for me.

I'll never forget it. The dizziness. The rails. A little more...a little more...

The light from the cabin...the faces in the train window...his arm tightening.

The rush of wind.

Just a little more.

The person you love, he holds you tight. You hold him tight. That's the proof.

But I should be talking about Susie P.

━━━ •

I don't know how Johnny did it, what he said to her. But they got together. Together, but not for real. Except for her, of course, it was very real. So real, she didn't even see that everyone was bent over laughing when they walked past, as a couple, in the hallway.

He held her hand. The whole time.

Sometimes he did things behind her back. He would walk along with one arm around her and be pressing a wad of chewing gum onto her ass with the other. Or he'd tell her the worst sort of bullshit and then turn around and make a face to his friends. He played with her, like a bored child plays with a toy it hates.

But it wasn't just him. We all played along.

And she kept turning up with even redder lipstick. How red can lipstick get?

A few days, a week, that's what they said. But the week became a month, and she still didn't get it. In fact, the more time passed, the more sure she was they were a couple. Nothing ever seemed to sink in— not the looks, not the laughing. She didn't even notice when people started making bets. It was unbelievable. They sent this list around so everyone in class could fill it out. You chose how long you thought it would take before Susie P. understood she'd been tricked. A month? Half a year?

Someone wrote "never." She will find out
NEVER. Really, what else could you believe?

▬▬▬ ●

Watching it made me feel sick. I mean—
who wouldn't? It was a natural reaction.
I thought he'd at least give me a sign.
A look or a word, something small that
would show me that we were still *us*.

But I didn't even get a look.

It was lonely. I didn't have anyone: just him.
I hadn't thought of that. I'd thought I had
friends who I could hang out with, but
now it was clear there was only him.

No one talked to me. I was on my own on the breaks. The kids in class started to giggle and stare whenever they saw me. As if it was suddenly me, and not Susie P., who was the big joke. *Where's your boyfriend?* they asked. *Got some competition?* Even though they knew exactly how things stood. It was supposed to be funny.

Pretty funny. Bunch of comedians.

I had trouble sleeping. There was too much to think about. Too many dark thoughts. Too much messing with my head. I couldn't relax.

Couldn't eat much, either.

"You're so pale," Mom said. "Your face is sunken in like a corpse's. Don't be like me and lose your fresh young skin too soon! A smile is the best makeup."

Shit!

Then I got angry. I mean, who did that shitface think he was? God or a king or something? I had other options. There were other guys who were interested.

One night I went into the woods and set fire to the stuffed animals—every single one of them—that he'd given me. Even the adorable tiger that was my favorite, the one he'd spent so much money on when

he was drunk and wanted to give me every-
thing. God, how it burned! WHOOSH!
Just, WHOOSH! It felt so good, so right...
The sparks were incredible.

I felt awful afterward. I couldn't understand
why I'd done it. I mean...he always wanted
to give me the most expensive, the cutest...
It's not very often that someone wants to
give you everything, is it? And I set fire to
it all.

I wondered if I was going crazy.
I decided to pull myself together. It was
hard, though, because I missed him so much.

We belonged together, I knew that. I was

the only one he could talk to, the only one who understood who he was. Who he was inside, in his heart. There was something special between us.

"A smile is the best makeup."

But it only got worse.

His friends—the pigs! They started to challenge him. They got him to do sick things with Susie P. "Kiss her!" they said. "Like hell I will." "Give you ten bucks if you do." "Twelve!" "Okay, but with your tongue, then." "Fifteen." "Okay." "Deal!" "But with your tongue! We'll be able to tell if you're cheating!"

And so he did. In the middle of the hallway.

With his tongue! Really! I'm not kidding.

"Touch her tits!" they said then. "Not on your life!" "Twenty bucks!" "No way—fifty, at least." "Dream on—twenty-five."

And so he did.

I had to do something. Should I tell her the truth? Just break it to her, right to her face? No, that wasn't a good idea. If I ruined the joke, Johnny would never forgive me—and then everything would be over between us anyway.

But one day—it was at the burger place—

I told her.

When I saw her sitting there on her own, I couldn't help myself.

"It's all a joke. *You're* the joke." That's what I said.

I could see she didn't want to believe me. She just sat there and giggled, studied me with those eyes, as if I was some kind of insect.

I wondered if there was something the matter with her. If there was something wrong with her brain. It sure seemed like it. She listened calmly to everything I said, but nothing seemed to sink in.

Then she said I was jealous. She said it was me—me!—not her that had the problem.

Those eyes—it made me completely furious when she looked at me like that! As if I was a piece of garbage...a speck of dust... nothing...

My mind went black. The only problem I had was her!

"It's you, it's you, it's you, *you're* the joke, Susie P."

I wanted to hit her. In the face. I came close.

━━ •

It wasn't that I couldn't get other guys. There were others who were interested. I've said that before and it's the truth. I could have had anyone if I'd really tried... Carson, Mario, any of them. It wasn't as if I was ugly or stupid or defective. That wasn't my problem.

It was because I was picky. Those other guys didn't do anything for me. A lot of them were jocks—not my type. And they didn't show any respect. They were always coming at you, always trying to kiss you or grab you, their hands all over you...not romantic at all.

Johnny wasn't like that. He was sensitive.

He had feelings. Some people thought he was cocky. But they didn't understand him. What did they know?

He always said that if someone was a bastard or didn't show me respect, I could come straight to him and he would take care of it.

What was the best thing he did? There was so much...but one thing I'll always remember. It was a winter day; it was snowing. It was really cold, minus twenty at least, and he pulled up the zipper on my jacket—all the way up—and said that I should keep warm and look after myself. It probably doesn't sound like a big thing to you, but it was for me. *You should keep warm and look after yourself.* It was nice. No one had ever treated me that way before.

But that was a long time before things started with Susie P.

Then the worst happened. It was just before Christmas.

It was at a party at school. I went up to Johnny and told him that enough was enough.

I didn't really expect him to listen. But at

first, it went okay. He told me that he missed me. He practically had tears in his eyes.

I told him he had to choose—her or me.

He said she was a joke and didn't mean anything to him.

But how would I know that, I said, the way he'd been carrying on?

"You have to give me something," I told him. "Some kind of proof. So I know you're serious about me."

I liked the sound of my voice when I said that. Cool and calm. It felt good. As if, finally, I had the power.

"What do you mean, proof?" he said.
"What kind of proof?"

I explained—in the same calm voice—that I couldn't know if he was serious about me until he did something to prove that he loved me. I think that was how I put it. Something that meant something, something really big.

He promised he would do something special for me.

Right after midnight they disappeared. I looked for them everywhere—on the dance floor, on the sofas, outside...

I don't know how long I looked. An hour.

Maybe more. I checked all the hallways,
fuming. I'd have to get home by myself.
I was about to give up when I heard the
sound.

It came from behind the door of one of
the classrooms. The chemistry room,
I think. I was the only one up there. I
stopped and listened. It sounded like—
how can I describe it? Like a kind of wail-
ing...very weak…and whimpering. I'd
never heard anything like it.

I knew I should get out of there, forget
everything I'd heard.

But instead, I opened the door.

She was lying there. And they were standing over her.

I stayed in the doorway, frozen in place.

Nobody said anything.

It smelled awful in that room. Alcohol, vomit...

Still I stood there. And she—

Susie P., for chrissake! You should...get up.

There were four of them. Him and his friends. I knew right away they had done something horrible. Because she was completely naked. Or almost. Right down to a pair of suede boots. My suede boots, the electric-blue ones.

I started screaming at him. *What the hell have you done? What have you done? What have you done? Did you steal my suede boots?*

She lay there, completely still...whimpering and staring straight at me with those eyes. Wanting me to do something. Help her, I suppose. But what could I do?

Johnny was standing there, his bare butt looking back at me.

Have you screwed her and given her my best boots? You asshole!

He turned to me and almost started to cry. Then he started saying a lot of sweet things, the sort of things he used to say before, before all this happened. His voice was quiet. "Baby, it's you and me, you know that. Forever. She doesn't mean anything. She's just a joke, a slut, she's nothing..."

Prove it, then!

"But that's what I'm doing! That's what I'm doing."

He said I could stay. Or leave. Whatever I wanted.

I stayed. I don't know why.

The four of them, including him, did
everything to her.

At first, one held her down while the others
did it. After that it wasn't necessary. She
just lay there—and stared straight at me.

That look... It was poison...it went straight
inside me, paralyzed me. I couldn't move,
could only stand there and watch while
they did it. While all four of them did it.

We didn't talk about it afterward. She
stayed away from school. A long time. It
was him and me again. I tried to forget
what had happened—tried to think about

something else. But it was still there. It never left.

It was a strange feeling. I knew what I had done was almost worse than the actual rape. Still, in some ways, I felt better than I had in ages. As if what had happened had brought us closer, Johnny and me. As if we shared something, and needed each other more than ever. It was wrong to think like that, I know—I'm the sort of person who often thinks the wrong thing—but that was what I thought.

Two cops came to get him. It was a Thursday night. He was arrested and taken to jail. They said she had reported him.

Someone else must have made her do it.
Her mother or someone. She would have
never done it herself.

He denied it. They called in several others
for questioning. But everyone stood by his
side—by our side. His and mine.

I was called. I denied it.

Then there was a hearing.

I sat in the front of the courtroom and
answered questions. It seemed as if the
people on the jury suspected she had
wanted it. I've heard guys say that some
girls like it rough. I think the jury took her
for one of those girls. Half the school was
there—her, too, of course.

She sat there with her mother, looking down.

Maybe she thought I would cave—now, when it really mattered—and tell the truth.

But I didn't.

I lied.

"I wasn't there. I didn't see anything."

"No... I don't know... No..."

"She's been in love with him forever. She'd been following him. Flirting..."

When I said that, she lifted her eyes and looked right at me. Her mouth opened and closed as if she was about to say something, or scream out loud, but then changed her mind.

It was strange. All I could think about, still, was my suede boots. No one had mentioned them...and I wanted to know how she got them and when I would get them back.

It bugged me. How could they keep a pair of such expensive boots and not give me anything for them? It was as if they didn't even care. As if she was the only person in the world who was important, the only person who meant anything now.

Johnny was all lit up afterward. Ecstatic. Everything had gone his way. When we came out of the hearing, he lifted me and twirled me around and called me his angel, his princess...sweet stuff like that.

At that moment, I didn't feel we had done anything wrong. I felt wonderful. We were back to being us. We had solved the problem, together. And we would never again, in our whole lives, be alone.

It all went as we had hoped. He was released. The others, too. They said there wasn't enough proof. "The proof of rape was not established." That's what they wrote in the newspaper.

She disappeared completely after that.

No one knew where to. There were rumors about a psych ward. But no one knew for sure when it came to Susie P.

I don't know what I was thinking back then. I probably thought I would forget. That the lie would fade and become less important in a few years.

But something like that doesn't disappear. It's as if... I don't know... You can sit in the park with the other mothers and talk about your kids and the things you're going to do on the weekend—go to the wave pool, maybe shop for some clothes—and it feels as if they know, as if they can see it in your eyes somehow. That you've done such an ugly thing. It's as if you're branded. As if you belong to another species and shouldn't be sitting there with the other mothers. As if you don't have the right.

I've tried to talk about this before...but it just felt embarrassing, wrong. I've never known who to tell. I don't know why I'm telling you.

Sometimes I think I see her. If I pass some person with problems...a drunk...some mental case who stands there shouting...a street person, I'm almost certain that it's her, that it *could* be her.

I destroyed her life. That's what I'm saying.

That's how it is.

━━━ ●

I don't know what more to say or what you must be thinking. But thank you for listening. It feels good to have told you.

I'm going home now. They're waiting. He's made dinner.

Just one more thing. I wasn't going to tell you this, but...we got married, Johnny and me. The day I turned eighteen. We've been together ever since. It will be seventeen years in March.

Our first child was a girl. Our second one, too. It's hard for me to describe how it's been for us. It's a kind of love, I suppose.

A kind of love.

What else could you call it?

Excerpt from

Caroline Adderson

Film Studies

There once was a girl who lay in bed for a long time every morning. In itself, this was hardly special. Most girls hate getting up. The alarm goes and they doze a bit, watching the light behind the curtains—is it raining or is it sunny?—until they figure out what to wear. But this girl was special. While she was drowsing in bed, she wasn't thinking about clothes. She was deciding which character to be that day. The Little Match Girl frantically striking matches to keep herself from freezing to death? No, she didn't feel *that* pathetic. The Ugly Duckling? That only worked when she had a pimple or something, because she was half-Danish and the Danes are beautiful. The Snow Queen?

No. She's been the Snow Queen too much lately.

Why do I do it? Why do I always need a role to play? My mother is, or was, an actress but I know I haven't inherited my dramatic tendencies from her. I'm not like Aurora at all. I get them from Erlend, my father, who is a film director. But his being a director is only part of the reason. It's also because he started reading the tales of Hans Christian Andersen to me when I was a tiny baby in his arms. Later, after he left, Aurora read them to me. And then, when I could, I read them to myself.

I don't know who to be today. Maybe the princess in the "Princess and the Pea" because I've been sleeping so badly. But being a princess would involve a prince. No thanks. There is no prince in my life. I never consort with the opposite sex except in the case of Erlend, who breezes into town once or twice a year.

Clem Martini

Too Late

What if you've done something so awful, your own parents don't even want you around?

I tell them I'll try to change, to be a good person. But they say it's too late.

So I'm stuck here in this nowhere place with guys who have no way out, just like me. I eat dinner, but don't taste it, attend group, but don't feel it. Get advice and pretend to take it, pretend to watch TV, pretend to sleep. It's all make-believe.

Now I hear they're about to make a registry of offenders like me and publish it wherever we go. So where do I head when I'm done here, and why pretend there's a point to any of this anyway?

Where do you go when there's nowhere left to run?

Single Voice

1 book | 2 stories

Two fearless explorations of the depths of teenage passion

NOTHING BUT YOUR SKIN
Cathy Ytak

Louella hates her name. She's obsessed with colors and when she gets upset, she yells herself hoarse. People call her "slow," but Lou knows one thing for sure: she wants to be with her boyfriend—no matter what her parents or doctors think. *Nothing but Your Skin* chronicles the aftermath of a mentally challenged girl's decision to have sex.

THE POOL WAS EMPTY
Gilles Abier

Sixteen-year-old Celia's boyfriend, Alex, is dead after falling into an empty swimming pool—and his mother has accused Celia of his murder. As Celia tries to clear her name and move on from her devastating loss, she reveals that the shocking events of that fateful day may not be what they seem.

Clem Martini

Too Late

Journal: Sept 5
I'm here. Six months
till I go home. You're
given me a tour, your
rules.

Annick Press Ltd.

Series editor: Melanie Little

Copyedited by Geri Rowlatt
Proofread by Tanya Trafford
Cover design by David Drummond/Salamander Hill Design
Interior design by Monica Charny
Cover photo (flashlight) by sming / shutterstock.com

We acknowledge the support of the Canada Council for the Arts, the Ontario Arts Council, and the Government of Canada through the Canada Book Fund (CBF) for our publishing activities.

ONTARIO ARTS COUNCIL
CONSEIL DES ARTS DE L'ONTARIO

Mixed Sources
Product group from well-managed forests, controlled sources and recycled wood or fiber
FSC www.fsc.org Cert no. SW-COC-002358
© 1996 Forest Stewardship Council

Annick Press is committed to protecting our natural environment. As part of our efforts, the text of this book is printed on 100% post-consumer recycled fibers.

Printed and bound in Canada by Webcom.

Published in the U.S.A. by
Annick Press (U.S.) Ltd.

Distributed in Canada by
Firefly Books Ltd.
66 Leek Crescent
Richmond Hill, ON
L4B 1H1

Distributed in the U.S.A. by
Firefly Books (U.S.) Inc.
P.O. Box 1338
Ellicott Station
Buffalo, NY 14205

Visit our website at www.annickpress.com

It's inside, hammering away. Bigger than panic. Bigger than my chest or my lungs. Squeezing. If I wait and I breathe, it slows down, but it always comes back. Since the meeting was set up, it's stayed longer. Each day, it's stronger.

It's crowding out all my other thoughts as I hike into the woods with two of the Garys: Gary Creavy and Gary Fontaine. Seems half the group is named Gary if you include

Gary Bonner, who's in our program and in solvent abuse, too. It's just after lunch so we've got twenty minutes. I'm listening to them with part of my brain—the other part is saying tomorrow, tomorrow, tomorrow.

The gravel path that runs alongside the cottages keeps going out into the deeper woods. Officially we're not supposed to smoke, but if we disappear into the bush, nobody objects. The path stretches a couple of miles through the forest preserve before it ends at a big wooden fence, rimmed with wire. I point out it wouldn't take much to climb it. Gary F. says, then what? As soon as you got out and away, they'd phone the cops. They catch you after you break parole,

you wind up in the joint. He looks at me. You wouldn't last two days there. They hate guys like us.

I'm not us, I say. Gary F. laughs, snaps his cigarette way off into the bushes. Yeah, he says. Keep saying that all you want. In the joint nobody's going to pay any attention to your explanation. The moment they find out what you did, they'll take you apart.

Smokes finished, we hike back. Cross the compound. Three wood cottages, a school, the mechanic's barn, an old brick admin building. It's so far out of the city that animals from the forest preserve sometimes stray in. Today I see a couple of skinny

rabbits shiver in the bushes as we pass
admin. A deer crossed the lawn yesterday.
Just before we get to the school I look over
at the coyote's skull that's nailed above the
door of the mechanic's barn. Tomorrow, it
says. Tomorrow.

▬▬ •

In through the big rusty, metal doors of
the school, down the hall to science class.
Meischmitt, the science teacher, fires up a
generator, runs electricity through random
pieces of metal, magnetizes them so that
things that didn't have a charge before
now cling together like their little metal
lives depend on it. Lit class, Mr. Danner

goes on and on about giants and dwarves
and old-time gods. For homework he tells
us to write out "the myth of me." I ask him
why, when everyone else at this place is
obsessed with what's true, he wants us to
write something that's a lie. He says it's
about finding other kinds of truths. Other
ways of thinking and feeling. I ask, isn't
that just like more group therapy? Because
I hate group therapy. He says maybe this
will change the way I feel. I don't think so,
I tell him. He says, who knows?—the gods
are pretty messed up, maybe even gods
have to do group. Screw that, I think. If
they're gods they got power. If they got
power they're for sure not doing group.

Back to Cottage C for dinner. I go to the
front desk, get my meds. Staff make sure
I swallow them. I ask, are there are any
messages yet? They say they'll let me know
when they hear. I ask, can I call? No. Can
I text? No. They remind me of my phone
suspension. I feel myself winding up. If you
touched me, I could snap like an elastic band.

I step outside, stand on the back porch with
my hands in my pockets. Look toward the
city. I figure her plane must have landed by
now. I wonder which hotel she's staying at.

▬▬ ●

Then it's time for group. We start with
some of the usual stuff. Behaviors and

strategies. Cycles of abuse. Gary F. begins talking about his grandfather. How the old man used to select which grandkid he'd do. How anyone who pushed him away would be punished. When Gary turned ten he made himself sick rather than have sex with his granddad. Next time he stayed over, the old man waited till everyone was asleep, crept in, tied Gary's sleeping bag shut, beat him with an extension cord till he lost consciousness. Gary talked about being trapped in that bag, struggling to get out. Begging and begging.

Suddenly it's so hot I'm sweating. The room's small and none of the windows will open. When session finishes and we're

dismissed I go outside, but it doesn't help. No matter what, I can't get enough air. I go out on the back porch looking for a breeze, then down the walk and across the lawn. My heart's pounding. Before I know it, I'm outside the compound.

We're not supposed to go past this point without permission but I keep going. I don't know where I'm heading, but a few more minutes and I'll reach the end of the road and the grocery store and the bus depot where you can get a bus into the city. And then what?

I see someone coming toward me. It's someone I know—the program's psychiatrist.

It's like I'm watching a movie—she's small, but with each step she's filling up more screen. I don't know how to avoid her. I don't know how to get past her, but I can't go back and if she tries to stop me I'll knock her to the ground. I don't care.

The psych doesn't try. She just walks next to me, like it's the most natural thing to do, even though she's going back the way she just came. She tells me she needs help and hands me a bag of groceries. I take the bag but tell her to leave me alone, tell her she's wasting her time walking in circles. She says she's got nothing against circles. We keep walking, me carrying her plastic bag. It's got coffee in it. I can smell it

through the foil wrap. She asks where I'm going. I still don't know. I'm shaking. She asks if I'm nervous about my six-month review. I tell her this place is messing me up, that I've got no future here. We walk.

"The future is a mystery," she tells me.

"So what am I doing?" I ask her.

"What do you mean?" she asks.

"Here. What am I doing here?"

"You'd know better than me," she says.

"The court ordered me here. But what for?"

"You're building something," she says.

"What?" I ask her.

"A flashlight," she says.

I don't even know what that's supposed to mean.

She says that when I've built my flashlight I'll shine it behind me to see where I've come from and eventually shine it ahead to see where I'm going.

I'm trying to figure that out and she loads me down with more stuff. "Help me," she says. "My arms are full."

I still don't have a place to go. For some reason it makes sense to go back, so we walk together and I help make coffee.

Lights out. Night climbs heavy on me, settles on my chest, hot. Then it's morning. But the hours still stretch out ahead. The meeting isn't until two.

Even more than usual, school just feels like a lot of random noise. People move past, their arms wag, their lips move, but nothing means anything. There's a morning assembly. Some guy who climbs mountains for a living tells us why climbing mountains made him a man.

I eat lunch, and two minutes after can't remember what it was. Someone at my table tells me they heard that my mom was on campus, but that she didn't stop at

the cottage. Later Brenda, the team leader, gets me from class and walks me to the conference room.

Mom and her man are seated already. She doesn't say a word—the Step Dud does all the talking. I can't take in what's going on at first. I'm just trying to get over the fact that we're all in the same room. Them over there, me over here. I haven't seen anyone from home since I was sent to this place. No phone calls all these weeks. No letters. Not even e-mail. Nothing.

I try to catch the expression on Mom's face. A smile, something. But there might as well be a million miles between us. It's

like she doesn't even remember me.

I sit still, but my blood's pounding and my hands are sweaty. I wipe them against my pant legs. Then my brain catches up to what's happening and suddenly I hear the Step Dud talking. His words pop out at me, clear. He's saying I've got to take ownership of my problem. Ownership of my problem? I ask. What does that mean? He just repeats it—as if the smallest child would know what it means. I hold my sweaty hands out in front of me.

I said I did it, I tell him. I confessed to the judge. I said I'm sorry. I said I won't do it again. I'm in therapy. What more can I do?

I tell them I wrote a letter to Deb to make restitution. The Step Dud says they haven't delivered the letter and won't.

What? What's that all about? I ask, and I'm trying to stay calm but I can feel my voice tightening.

Our choice, says the Step Dud, using his lecturing voice. We did what we felt was best.

It was my letter, I tell him, getting louder. My letter to her for her to read.

She's in our care, he says, and she's been through enough. We don't want to scare her, he says.

So what am I supposed to do? I ask.

They don't say anything. I ask again, and when I don't get an answer I ask again.

My mother stands, pushes her chair back, leaves the room. The program coordinator runs after her. Step Dud goes out too. Something in the way he swats the door shut says he can't decide who has annoyed him more, me or Mom. Meeting over, I guess. I sit, me and the random empty chairs. Brenda talks low to someone from admin in the corner.

Another meeting's scheduled for tomorrow.

—— •

Tonight when I try sleeping, every day of the last six months flips past. I think about all the time I've spent in program. I think about tomorrow and the next day, and the days after that, stretching ahead of me like train tracks.

I wake. This meeting is set for right after breakfast, so I don't have to go to school. I head up to admin again, but this time when I step into the conference room everything's changed. The furniture is moved, the seats are arranged in a big happy circle, and it's full of all kinds of people who weren't here yesterday. My case worker's here. My parole officer's here. The

psych is here, the director of the program's here, and way, way off on the other side, my mother and the Step Dud. My mother is crying.

Sheila, the program director, waits for Mom to get it together. That's not in the cards so Sheila launches into things while Mom blots at her face with a soggy tissue. Sheila mouths something about everyone having their say, something else about re-spect for feelings, but in the end it comes down to one thing—they won't take me back. They say I'm too big a risk.

I just sit there for a minute, trying to make sense of it, but I can't.

It's like—with one decision—every part of me before I was sent to the program has been erased, like I never had a grandma or cousins or friends, like I never had a home.

The Step Dud I could see, but my own mother?

They say they have to make it safe for my stepsister and can't risk having me there. She's been in the house only a year, right? But it's her this and her that.

"What about me?" I say. The Step Dick says, "You had your chance."

"When? When did I have my chance? Who kept things safe for me when it was

my dad at home?" Mom won't even meet my eyes.

I tell them I'm sorry, that I won't do it again. They say no one trusts me anymore. So I'm fucking bawling now, and I can't stop. "I'll be good," I tell them. "I'll be good." Step Dick walks outta the meeting again, and this time the door clicks shut like that's his final statement. My mom keeps crying, saying, "It's too late to be good."

Too late to be good.

━━━ ●

So that's it, I'm done. They'll send for my things, put them in storage. I'll complete treatment and find another placement, if there is another placement. If anyone will take me. And I'm thinking about closed doors, the closed door at the end of Cottage B with the cartoon that's taped on it of Death in a black robe, holding his scythe in one hand, distributing questionnaires with the other that ask, "Tell me how I'm doing today." I'm thinking of my hometown and how that's just another kind of closed door now. I'm thinking about the coyote skull nailed to the mechanic's barn, and now I know what it was grinning about. It knew yesterday that the door was about to slam shut.

And Otis, I'm thinking about him too. He
finished program here, turned eighteen,
funding over. They gave him an independent
living placement in his hometown back
east. So far so good, right? But the news-
papers found out he was back and published
his name and his address. Someone shot
out his window one night. His neighbors
marched in front of his apartment building.
The landlord canceled his lease. People
were pushing, shouting, throwing things,
so the police picked him up, took him to
the airport, and stuffed him on a plane.
He's here again, living in the facility, and
nobody knows what to do with him or
where to send him. I read that they're

going to make a national registry of sex
offenders and publish it wherever we go.
So where do I go when I'm done, and why
pretend there's a point to treatment?
I eat dinner, but don't taste it, attend
group, but don't feel it. Pretend to watch
TV at quiet time, get advice from the staff
and pretend to take it, pretend to sleep. It's
all make-believe.

I wait a day, cause I know they'll keep a
close watch on me for a day at least. I go
to my classes. Mr. Danner hassles me for
my "myth of me" assignment. I tell him

everything about me is made up. He says
I can do better than that. Gives me an
extension. The next night, after lights out,
I throw my things in a bag, leave by the
back door. I sell my iPod to Leslee up at
Spiritlives Program. She meets me at her
window, I pocket the cash and go.

The grounds are deserted. I cross the lawn,
cut through the forest. It's dark, but I follow
the path by feel, by the sound of the gravel
under my feet. A couple of miles in, I scale
the fence and start to climb the hill. But it's
pitch black now and I can't see how to make
my way through the bush. I try fighting
through it. Branches snag me. Thorns
slash me. I trip, fall back, slide down the

hill, rip my jacket. My bag falls and gets
lost in the underbrush. I kneel and reach
into my pocket, take out my lighter, set fire
to a dead branch, and use it as a torch.
After that it's better. I'm like one of Mr.
Danner's gods. Climbing the hill, I feel the
heat on the back of my hand, the branch
crackling, lighting up the ground ahead of
me. I find my way to the top. From there a
long rippling field of tall grass stretches to
the highway, hissing and whispering. I think
about setting fire to the grass. Setting the
whole hillside on fire. Burn my tracks, burn
my history, burn every trace that I was here,
leave nothing behind, nothing but ash and
smoke and embers. I want to. But at the

same time I know if you set fire to something, you send a signal and everything
comes. Fire department, police department,
every other kind of department. I snuff my
torch on a rock and throw the smoking
branch spinning into the bushes. The
night sky whirls above me, and suddenly I
feel like I'll fall off the earth if I don't hold
on. I grab handfuls of dirt, wait, crouched,
till the dizziness passes. Then I stand,
wade through the tall grass to the side of
the highway, and stick out my thumb.

━━ ●

Cars blow past. I keep watch for police.

After forty-five freezing minutes, I finally get my first ride. Wouldn't you know it: a mom and dad, all concerned, asking me if I'm lost. I tell them I'm returning home. Never was a bigger lie, but it's the right answer, I guess, because they give me a ham and cheese sandwich from a package they'd put together for their drive. They let me off an hour later.

Next, some guy in a beat-up Mustang, big droopy 'stache. Doesn't say a word, pulls over after forty minutes, nods for me to get out. Then a man chain-smoking, lighting his cigarettes one off the other, asking me to talk and keep him awake. Then a truck driver. Then a red Toyota with a thin man

and a dog. The dog is stuffed into a small cage in the back. The man peppers me with questions as the dog whines nervously. How old are you, how many brothers, how many sisters? I turn, the dog has its muzzle pressed between the wires, tongue lolling red and eyes open wide. It's a husky-shepherd cross, the man tells me. Its long ears bend into two furry Ts as its head presses against the top of the cage. It stares through the wires right into me. The man says it's for the dog's own good. The cage will protect him. The cage will keep him safe. I hear him telling me that, but I've never seen a cage that kept anyone safe, and I see the wire cutting into the fur and wonder what

the dog thinks. The man drives and fires
questions faster than I can think. Plans for
the future? he asks me. No idea. What
skills have you got? None. What do you
want to be? Nothing. You must want to be
something? No. Want to grow up to be
something? No. Everyone's got skills they've
been given, he insists, everyone has gifts.
It's like he won't stop, and in the end I snap.
There are no gifts. There's nothing I've got
that anyone wants. After that the ride gets
quiet. A little while later he lets me out.

Two hours in the dark, the wind rising. A
lot of time, just me and the road. Time to
think about whether I'll get caught. If I don't
get caught, what will I do next? I stamp to

keep warm and hum a song I only half
remember. The wind snatches up the part
I remember along with the part I don't.
The cold feeling I've got in my fingers and
feet moves in deep, settles in my belly.

I hear a police siren. They can't know
which direction I've gone yet, but if they
pull over, they'll ask for ID and if they do,
I'm finished. I grab my bag, scramble up
the slope beside the road, crouch among
the trees in the dark, and watch. I think
back to all the times in my life I've spent
hiding. In the closet, in the basement, in
the dust that settled under the back steps,
under dirty clothes in the laundry, in the
trunk of the car, hiding till everyone was

gone, till folks passed out, till the old man was asleep. I'm the hiding expert. I wonder about Toyota Man and his questions, wonder what kinds of jobs call for expert hiding skills? The police car wails louder as it draws close. I wait till the wail fades to a whisper, then stand up and stumble back down through the brush.

It's deep morning now. Practically nobody's driving along the road—it's just a bare, thin strip of pavement and me. Nothing else to do, so I walk, I don't know how far.

I hear a soft whir, turn and see lights like

tiny eyes appear at the farthest end of the valley. The dim headlights approach and I stick out my thumb. A pickup slows, then stops. Two older guys in a rusty green half-ton. The driver's window is cranked down and I meet Dusty and—can you believe it?—another Gary. Seems like the whole world can't get enough of Garys.

I open the rear door and squeeze into the crew cab. It's a tight fit because there's blankets and equipment and two cases of beer on the floor. The cab's warm and smells a little of something. I figure it must have something to do with the plastic sandwich pack of hash lying on the seat in front. Dusty glances back at me and asks,

"You on the run from something?" I say, a
little. Dusty nods and says, "Been there."
And just by looking at him I can see that
he has. Guys like us are like those magnet-
ized metal pieces in science class, somehow we find and cling to each other.

"Crank up the tunes," Gary says, and
Dusty does. "Knock the caps off some beer.
You got work on the coast?" Dusty asks me.
I tell him not yet. "Anything in particular
you looking for?" "Whatever," I say, "so
long as it pays." "Might know something,"
he says. He tells me he's heard where there's
a kick-ass bush party. I'll meet people there.
We drink to it, drain our cans, open fresh
ones. Drive up a winding back road. Park

at the far end of some rocky nowhere. We
stand outside, wait, kill the beers, holler,
toss the empties high, whistling into the
darkness, turn up the tunes as far as they'll
go. Everything's good.

One of them, Dusty maybe, fires up a
blowtorch they keep in the back of the truck
and we crush the hash between two red-
hot caulking knives, suck the explosion of
smoke in through an oily metal funnel. I
think how easy this do-over has been. How
I've left the cottages, the programs, and
the disposable me behind and am halfway
to becoming the new me. The new me
that has nothing to do with anxiety attacks

or writing letters or sitting in group sessions remembering bad times. I reach into the truck, open and drain another can.

Then I notice Gary's leaning against me, pushing—to get another beer, I guess. I shift over, but he's grinding up against me again, pushing up against me and I'm pushing back, telling him, "Wait a minute, get off!" but I'm too wasted to do much good. He knocks me backward into the cab, yanks up my shirt, and starts groping. I can't get him to stop and he's too heavy to move. My jeans come down. I head-butt him but it's like head-butting bubble wrap. I try again. He bites me over the eye, then presses on my arms and shifts his

weight onto me. I pull one hand free, grab a fold of flab, and bite. While he's shouting, I squirm out from under him but Dusty has crowded the doorway like a goalie minding the net. He thumps me on the side of the neck, and when I drop to my knees thumps me again on the back of my head with the broken end of a hockey stick. I must have still been moving because he gets agitated and whacks me a couple more times and I check out.

I wake what must be only a couple moments later and realize I'm bleeding hard enough that it scares them. They shovel me into the back of the cab, cover me with a dirty blanket, fire up the motor, and take off.

We're bumping back down the road. I
don't know where they're going. I don't
know if I'm going to live. I can feel the
blood pooling under my head. When we
get back on the highway I figure it's now
or never and I kick the door open and roll
out. I hit the gravel by the side of the road
and bounce like a beer can tossed from the
window. Bang, bang, bang, clunk.

I scramble to my feet and run for the trees
off the highway. I didn't have to worry,
though, they're done. The truck keeps
right on motoring.

I must have snapped the little finger on my right hand in the roll-out or in the earlier wrestle. There's a lump on the back of my head and a deep gash that won't close, it just keeps oozing blood. I watch for someone to flag down, but no dice. I'm freezing and can't figure out where else to go. Everything I touch is dust, everything I touch crumbles, everything I do goes wrong. I limp along the highway until I come to a side road that leads down into the valley.

I follow it, stumble into a shabby mountain town in my muddy, bloody underwear, turn myself in to the police. They enter my name in their electronic registry, run me over to the local clinic where I get my hand taped,

my nose taped—it got busted at some
point—stitches to the back of my head
and where Gary bit off the end of my
right eyebrow. The cops give me some
stiff, scratchy inmate stuff to wear. Put me
in a holding cell back at the station. The
next day, the city cops arrive to pick me up.
The door to my unit opens, and a tall uni-
form say let's go, and repeats it when I
don't stand fast enough.

I crawl into the back of the car and we drive.
Everything I passed on my way out, I pass
again. Everything I thought about before,
I think about again, only even more edged
in acid this time. I watch the landscape:
trees then rocks then trees then rocks.

I remember an argument I had with my psych when I first entered the program. She said if I let them, my peers could help me deal with my problems. I told her they're not my peers. I'm not the same as them. I had a deal with the court. I agreed to take treatment. Charges were dropped.

She said they weren't dropped, only modified because of my age.

"Whatever," I said.

She kept going.

"You're here because you confessed to sexual assault—"

"Assault," I said. "Not sexual assault, I never agreed to sexual assault."

"You forced her down."

"We were fighting."

"Her shirt was undone."

"It came open."

"You were on top of her, she was undressed. What do you think that felt like for her?"

"I'm not a mind reader," I said.

She stared hard at me, said, "I'm not asking you to be a mind reader. I'm asking you to

demonstrate empathy. Your stepsister says
you pressed yourself against her. She says
you covered her face to keep her from calling, that she felt you were smothering—"

"That's a lie," I told her, and I stood up.
"That's a lie."

She was still seated in her fancy psych
chair, still making like she was calm. "You
didn't have your arm over her face?"

"We were fighting!" I shouted. "Do you
know what fighting is? I might have tried
to keep her from calling out, but that's all."

"Were you afraid she would call out?"

"Afraid?" I wasn't afraid—I knew. Of course Deb was going to call out. Since she and the Step Dud came, two pieces of the same package, that's all she's done. She calls, he comes, and I'm the disposable nothing. And all at once the answer to Toyota Man's question comes to me. Those are my skills, that's what life has trained me to do. I wanted to punish her the worst way I knew how, and I did. I wanted her to feel bad and small and worthless. I wanted her to feel what I'd felt, to know what I knew. Mission accomplished.

We're nearing the city, past the city limits, in the city center, at remand. I'm asked for my name though they already have it and

my birth date though they must have that too. I breached parole, so I spend three weeks in segregation.

━━━ ●

Let me tell you: time on your own bites if you're the last person you want to spend time with. Minutes drag and the weeks are sandpaper, wearing away a little more with each pass. You'd think I'd be hungry, but I can't be bothered to eat. Staff make more meetings for me—seems like they can't make enough—meetings for psychiatric assessment, meetings with a doctor, meetings with Sheila and with Brenda from Cottage C, meetings with a judge and a

lawyer and a social worker. Finally they
put me back into care and transfer me out
of remand over to stabilization for secure
treatment. They're watching me, afraid I'll
run again, but where would I run to?

There's no place to go.

You wanted the myth of me, Mr. Danner?
Here it is.

I was born in the dark, and have lived in
the dark every day of my life.

Everything I've ever had has been stolen.

I'll tell you who I am.

I'm those dwarves you talked about, buried underground, hammering away but never getting anywhere.

And I'm the giants too, and every day I want to knock something over, tear something apart, beat the shit outta someone.

And I'm a ghost, so dead, for so long, I don't even know what spell or potion you'd use to call me up.

━━ ●

The psych visits. Not sure which day. I'm still in pajamas, and the pajamas hang off me because I've lost so much weight.

They're still afraid I'm going to run again, so they won't let me have real clothes or shoes or slippers even. I tell her to go away, but psychs don't speak the same language as the rest of the world. Instead she sits beside me on my bed. Hauls a big photo album onto her lap. Says look at these photos with me.

I look. It's the family album they had me put together when I first came into the program. All these pictures of my family at the old home. The real family. Dad, my real dad. Buzz cut. Sharp chin, sharp nose. Sharp edges on everything. Mom hovering in the background, out of frame and out of focus. Like a ghost. And me. I come up to

the old man's waist. Skinny neck, skinny body, big ears.

━━ ●

The psych asks me how old I think I was when my dad started in on me. I flip the page back and forth a couple of times. I tell her it was about then, about that age, about when I was five.

I look at it. I look at us.

I'm standing next to him, he's got his big bony hand draped on my shoulder. It's like I'm a dwarf in a land of giants. She asks me, "What could you have done?"

"What do you mean?" I say.

"What could you have done to stop him?"

I stare at the grainy photos. I remember the height when he lifted me, the smothering weight when he pressed against me, the sick fear and the days spent looking out the window.

"Nothing," I tell her.

I could have done nothing.

She stays longer but the rest of the visit goes through and past me. Danner, you said the whole point of telling our stories is to make us think. Don't you get that I don't want to

think? When I think, I think what the
fuck is up with my life? Everything and
everyone I know are so completely totally
screwed that if I start down that road, it
grinds me to nothing. What good does
thinking do if all it does is make us nuts?

▬ •

And the psych—she shows me these photos
of me and my family and my dad, tells me
I'm not responsible for what happened when
I was little, and thinks that's supposed to
make me feel good? Yeah? Good how,
exactly? Good that I couldn't do anything
to stop him? Good that my life has been

poison? I get up. I open my cupboard, pry off the wall at the back, and take out the bottle I jacked earlier in the day. I pop the lid, drink the Javex. The sharp smell of the bleach catches at the back of my throat, and I have to make sure I don't breathe in as I swallow. It burns as it goes down and I want to throw up but I swallow and swallow and I feel it scalding my throat, scorching my nostrils, killing me from the inside out, just the way I want it to. Staff are knocking at the door but I don't answer and I've jammed it shut. They knock harder and shout, then break down the door. They haul me up, throw me in a car, drive me to the hospital. I puke in the car, and puke

again on the pavement outside emergency. The nurses tell me they pumped my stomach, but I don't know cause I blacked out and didn't wake up till the next morning, and here I am in the psych ward. My mouth is burnt, my throat is scarred, and all I'm thinking is that except for the details, everything my father said, I said. Everything my father did, I did. We're exactly the same.

Exactly the same.

═══ ●

The next day, the psych comes by the hospital, asks how I'm feeling. I don't answer

because really, given everything, what kind
of question is that? She says what I did the
other night was healthy—it's amazing how
psychs can make anything bad seem good
and anything good seem bad. She says I
arrived at an epiphany. I have her spell it.

She says it means an important realization.
She says she doesn't agree with how I reacted
to my epiphany, but says I could never have
started healing without it.

Right. And what that means I don't know.

She says I'll feel bad for some time but I'll
have to be strong. I don't know about the
strong part, but she's right about feeling

bad. All this time I spent hating my dad, and I am my dad. I'm him, except younger.

━━ ●

I'm sent back to Cottage C for more treatment with Rick, Otis, and the three Garys. On campus, everybody hears everything so they all know about my AWOL, my failed escape, my failed suicide, all my failures.

Turns out I've arrived just in time for some big performance based on Mr. Danner's myths unit. Danner's been making the guys act, and there's a lot of running around getting ready. It almost makes me glad I was in solitary all that time.

We sit outside at sunset, on the west lawn
between the cottages and admin. The guys
are dressed as old-time gods with cloaks
and spears and cardboard lighting bolts,
only they're sitting in chairs, just like we
do in group, trying to work out their shit,
all the mayhem and craziness and bad
behavior that gods get up to. And it's all
make-believe, and the acting is totally
crappy and there's nothing real, but I end
up crying and don't know why. I have to
grab a napkin from the snack table to get
straightened up. If anyone asks I'll tell
them I was trying like hell not to laugh.

By the time the play's done, stars have
started to come out and bugs and dragon-
flies. Bats zigzag overhead. All the social

workers and psychs stand up from their folding chairs to clap, and all of the moms and dads and foster moms, too. They're all there, with the exception of mine.

The guys get flowers and hugs from Brenda. There are little wrapped presents for each of them, too, chocolates and candies and stuff. I'm just happy to be wearing shoes and real pants again.

I look out across the grounds. There's the lawn. There are the trees beyond the lawn, and the shadows between the trees. I know I can run again. And part of me is wondering how far and how fast, and another part is thinking as far as I get, as fast as I go, everything catches up and the running

is easy, but the getting caught up to is a son of a bitch.

Then the bugs start to bite, and people move inside with their snacks and fruit punch. I decide to wait for a while. I fold and stack the chairs along with Gary F., but really I'm back inside my own head again. I'm watching the bats dart across the night sky. I know bats are nearly blind, I read that somewhere. Still, they get where they have to get with no light, no maps or help. Maybe you don't need a flashlight. Maybe there's more than one way to find your way in the dark.

Billie Livingston

The Trouble
with Marlene

I used to lie awake till two or three in the morning and think of the easiest ways to die: eating Drano (in gel capsules so it'd just slip down), electrocution (blow-dryer in the bathtub), fast-moving truck (stepping in front of). On a talk show I saw a few months back, a woman told about how her son died by autoerotic asphyxiation. He hanged himself with a necktie in his closet, accidentally suffocating while he jerked off over a porno mag. I wouldn't

need any of that, just the tie.

I probably sound like a major psycho. Maybe I am. But if I am then it runs in the family. My mom thinks about killing herself all the time lately. Except Marlene thinks it out loud. It's crazy. She used to be so cool—and I was her kid so I felt like it rubbed off on me in a way. Not so long ago, it was her and me against the world. Now look at us: a pair of defectives. How did we get this way?

It's Sam's fault, the way I figure it. If my dad hadn't screwed up, he wouldn't have landed in jail and they never would have split up. And if my parents hadn't split up,

we wouldn't have been so broke and if we hadn't been broke Marlene never would have tried the bullshit con-job that sent her off the rails in the first place.

I am sitting on the edge of Marlene's bed, watching her breathe. Watching her gives me a weird buzz in my guts, like a bee in a jar.

Vincent Karle

Descent into Paradise

It's my fault.

What happened—I didn't want it to, but it happened anyway, and now it's too late to fix it.

They came to look for me, but it was him they took away, and I'm still here.

Now I'm alone. As for him—I don't know where he is.

His name is Zaher.

That's Afghani.

My name's Martin.

At first, I didn't like him.

It's not that he wasn't cool, it's not that he was foreign; it's just that nobody knew him. He came to Paradise after the school year had started. He looked like he'd just gotten off the boat from Afghanistan— people said that his family had fled the war. He ended up in our class, and he had a sister who went to the kindergarten next door.